The Bog Baby

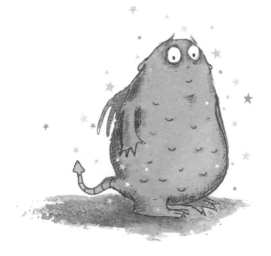

Written by Jeanne Willis   Illustrated by Gwen Millward

schwartz & wade books · new york

For my mother, xxx — J.W.
For Mum and Dad, with love — G.M.

Text copyright © 2008 by Jeanne Willis
Illustrations copyright © 2008 by Gwen Millward

All rights reserved. Published in the United States by Schwartz & Wade Books,
an imprint of Random House Children's Books, a division of Random House, Inc., New York.
Originally published in paperback in Great Britain by Puffin Books, an imprint of the Penguin Group, London, in 2008.
Schwartz & Wade Books and the colophon are trademarks of Random House, Inc.

Visit us on the Web! www.randomhouse.com/kids
Educators and librarians, for a variety of teaching tools, visit us at www.randomhouse.com/teachers

Library of Congress Cataloging-in-Publication Data is available upon request.
ISBN 978-0-375-86176-5 (hardcover) — ISBN 978-0-375-96176-2 (lib. bdg.)
The text of this book is set in Old Claude.
MANUFACTURED IN CHINA

10 9 8 7 6 5 4 3 2 1
First U.S. Edition

$\mathcal{L}$ong ago, when we were little, me and Chrissy did something bad.
We said we were going to Annie's house to play, but we didn't.

We went fishing. All by ourselves.
Which wasn't allowed.
Chrissy said there was a *magic pond in Bluebell Wood.

It was only ever there in spring.
    When it rained, it made a huge puddle in the dell,
and pond creatures came. We could fish for newts, she said.
                    I won't tell if you won't. So we went.

We found the pond.
 It was squelchy
  around the edge.
The bluebells squeaked under our boots.

We fished
and
fished,
but we didn't catch a newt.

We caught something much better.

We caught a **Bog Baby**.

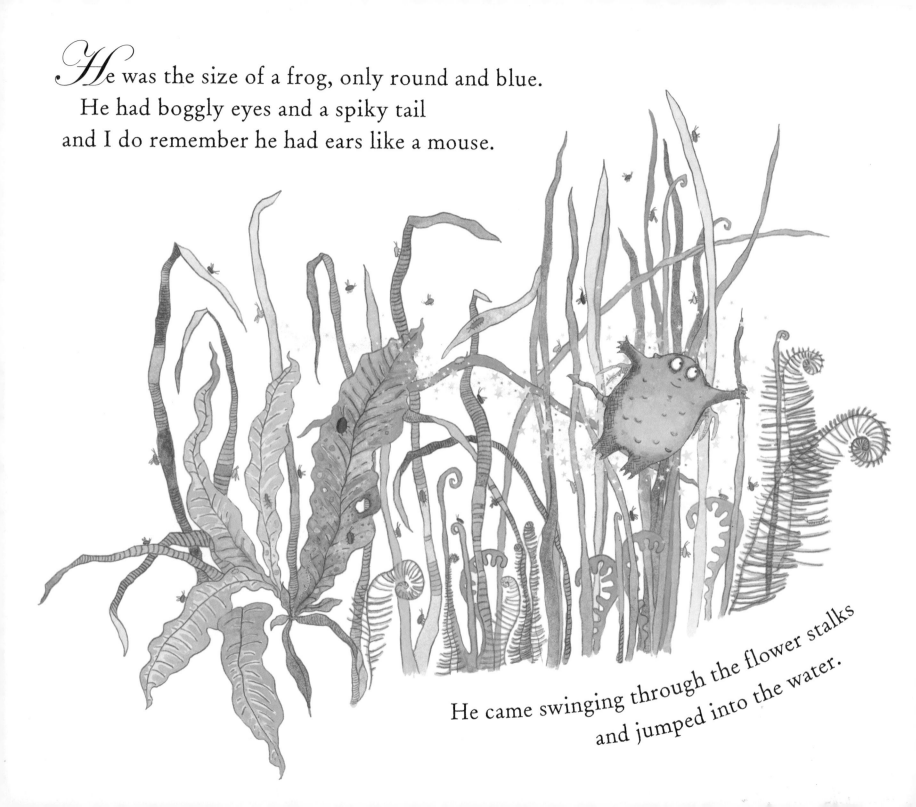

He was the size of a frog, only round and blue.
He had boggly eyes and a spiky tail
and I do remember he had ears like a mouse.

He came swinging through the flower stalks
and jumped into the water.

He floated up and down on his
back and sucked his toes.

That's when I fished him out.

He didn't struggle.

He sat in my hand and
looked surprised.

He was as soft as jelly.

Like he had no bones.

When we stroked him, he flapped his wings.
They were no bigger than daisy petals.
They seemed too small for him to fly.

Chrissy said he might be able to fly
if we *blew* on his wings.

We *blew* and *blew,* but all we did was blow him onto the mud.
He didn't try to escape. He just sat still with his paws over his eyes.

We put him in a jam jar, took him home and hid him in the shed.

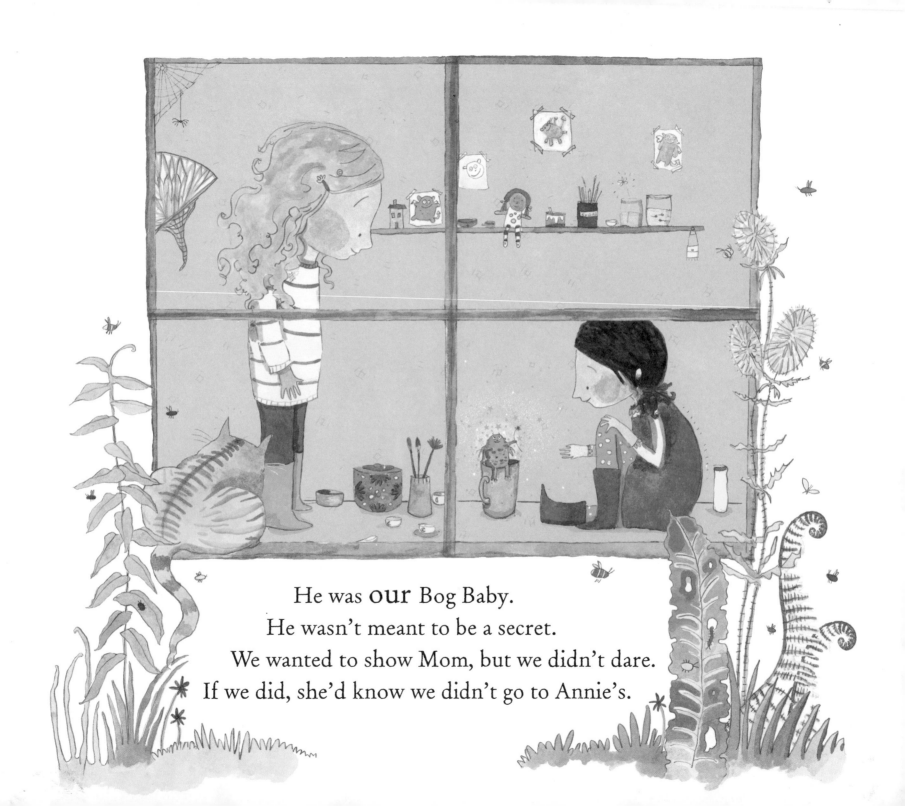

He was **our** Bog Baby.
He wasn't meant to be a secret.
We wanted to show Mom, but we didn't dare.
If we did, she'd know we didn't go to Annie's.

We made our Bog Baby
a beautiful home in a bucket.

Gravel.

Shells.

Clean water.

Whenever he saw us,
he jumped up and down.
We picked him up and
played with him.

He was very ticklish.
We fed him cake crumbs.

We loved our Bog Baby.

Our friends loved him too. We sneaked him into school in a margarine tub. When the teacher wasn't looking, he played in the sandbox.

In the afternoon, he slept in his tub on some damp cotton balls.

Chrissy made him a collar and leash and we took him for
walks in the field. Once, a crow almost ate him,
but we scared it away just in time.

We took great care of our Bog Baby.
At least, we tried. But he got sick.

He didn't jump up and down anymore.
He turned pale and his wings drooped.

He wouldn't touch his cake crumbs.
We gave him all sorts, but he spat them out.

We wanted to ask Mom for help, but we didn't dare.
Because of Annie.

But the Bog Baby got thinner.
He wouldn't walk on his leash.
He hid under his shell.

He wouldn't come out, no matter how much we loved him.

Mom found us in the shed.

Chrissy wouldn't say why we were crying.
We'd promised not to tell, but I blabbed.
Mom wasn't angry, though.

When she saw who was in the bucket, she smiled and her eyes went misty.
She said she hadn't seen a Bog Baby since she was little.

Please make him better, we cried.
We love him **so much**.

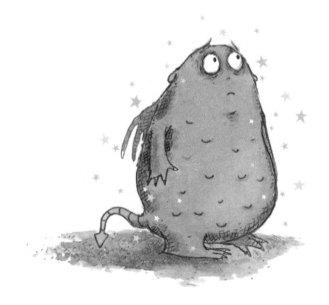

I know, she said.
But the Bog Baby is a wild thing.
He doesn't belong here.
He isn't meant to eat cake.
Or walk on a leash.
Or sleep in a tub.

She picked up
the bucket and we
followed her out.

If we really loved
the Bog Baby, we had to
do what was best for him.
No matter how much it hurt us.

That was **real love**.
That's why we let him go.

Back where he belonged.

Living in the woods.
Playing in the pond.
Sleeping in the damp leaves under the moon.

We never saw him again.
I think he grew up and had babies of his own.

Last spring, my daughter found the
*magic pond, and guess what she saw . . .

Hundreds of Bog Babies swinging through the bluebells.

Catching flies.

Floating on their backs.

Sucking their toes.

That's what she told me.
And that's what I believe.

Notes about your Bog Baby

When you find your very own Bog Baby, you can write all about him here.

Where did you find him? . . . .

What is his favorite food? . . . .

How many toes does he have? . . . .

What is his favorite flower? . . . .

Does he croak, purr or tweet? . . . .

Bog Babies are extremely rare. Very little is known about them. If you are lucky enough to find one,
it would be helpful if you could make notes and a small sketch and send them to S.O.B.B. (Save Our Bog Babies)
at the following address: Schwartz & Wade Books, Random House, Inc., 1745 Broadway, New York, New York 10019.